THE BIG HOUSE AND THE LITTLE HOUSE

THE BIG HOUSE AND THE LITTLE HOUSE

By YOSHI UENO   Pictures by EMIKO FUJISHIMA

LEVINE QUERIDO

MONTCLAIR · AMSTERDAM · NEW YORK

On a gentle slope rose a long, long road. At one end was a little house, standing all alone.

At the other end of the road was a big house, surrounded by trees.

Next to the little house was a beautiful river. Little Mouse lived there, all alone.

Next to the big house was a big oak tree. Big Bear lived there all by himself.

Every morning Little Mouse went to town.

At the same time Big Bear went
to the forest walking the opposite way.
And that's why the two of them had
never met.

Little Mouse worked at a bakery. The days were busy, no time to chat!

Big Bear worked alone in the forest.
There was no one to eat lunch with.

One Sunday, Little Mouse decided to
go to the forest.
"Maybe I will meet someone there!"
Mouse said.

Big Bear decided to go to town.
"How wonderful if I could meet
someone nice there!" said Bear.

Little Mouse hurried to the forest and Big Bear
scurried to town. They both looked straight ahead
and they didn't even notice each other!

The forest on Sunday was full
of animals enjoying picnics.
"I'm the only one who is all
alone," Little Mouse thought.

The town on Sunday was lively and crowded with cheerful animals, chatting and laughing.

"I'm the only one who is all alone," Big Bear thought.

Big Bear hung his head
and walked home.
  "I feel so lonely."

Little Mouse walked home,
looking up to the sky.
  "I feel so lonely…"

In front of Big Bear's house, their eyes met.

"He…hello…"

"Hello…"

"…Er…I live here…and I always drink tea alone. Wou…would you like to have a cup of tea with…?" Big Bear asked.

"Yes, I would love to have a cup of tea. Just right now I'm quite thirsty," Little Mouse answered.

Little Mouse entered Big Bear's big and cozy house. She took a seat on a tea cup on a big table and drank tea from a little milk jug.

"This table is bigger than my house. It's great to drink tea in such a spacious home!" Little Mouse said.

"You are my first guest ever. It's great to drink tea with a guest!" Big Bear said.

They talked about
all they thought and felt.
About the town and the
forest. About how things
used to be, and the good
and bad of how things are now.
They even talked about their
wishes. . . .

Bear and Mouse had a
great time together, but
soon it was time to go home.

"Goodbye," said Bear.
"Can we meet again?"
"Yes!" said Mouse.
"How about next Sunday."

Next Sunday it was raining and the wind grew fierce.
Big Bear was worried.
"Can we meet if it's such bad weather?"

But the sky grew dark and the rain dashed against the windows.

"It's a storm! Little Mouse's house is next to the river. What if the river bursts its banks? I have to help!"

Big Bear rushed into the
storm along the long, long road.

"ARE YOU OK?" shouted Bear.
"Yes!" said Mouse. "But the storm will
wreck my house! What can we do?"

The river looked as if it could burst its banks any second. "Don't worry, Little Mouse, I have an idea. Hold tight!" yelled Big Bear.

"Okay, Big Bear. Be careful!" shouted Little Mouse from inside.

Big Bear ran through the raging
storm while around him it was pitch dark.

Big Bear's shoulder began to hurt
as the house was very heavy. But he
continued running, calling out:
"Everything will be fine Little Mouse.
Just don't lean out of the window."

Big Bear put Little Mouse's
little house carefully next to
his big house.

"I hope you like this spot,
Little Mouse," Big Bear said.
"The oak tree will keep your
house dry."

Little Mouse came outside
and smiled.
"Thank you, Bear. That's
an excellent spot."

In Bear's big house, at
the cozy table, Big Bear and
Little Mouse drank a cup of hot tea.
"Today was a stressful Sunday,
wasn't it?"
"But we met."

And so it came to be that
the big house and the little house
lived next to each other. Every
morning Little Mouse and
Big Bear said "Good morning!"
to each other and went to work.
Little Mouse to town, and
Big Bear to the forest.

In the evening, they talked about
all the things that happened that day.
And neither was lonely anymore.

This is an Em Querido book
Published by Levine Querido

LQ

LEVINE QUERIDO

www.levinequerido.com · info@levinequerido.com

Levine Querido is distributed by Chronicle Books LLC

Originally published in Japan in 2012 as
Ōkii Ouchi to Chîsai Ouchi
by IWASAKI Publishing Co., Ltd., Tokyo.

Library of Congress Control Number: 2020937585
ISBN 978-1-64614-049-7

Printed and bound in China

Published in March 2021
First Printing

Book design by Christine Kettner
The text type was set in P22 Mayflower

To create the artwork for this book, Emiko Fujishima
first drew rough sketches of each scene.
Then, on illustration boards, she began line drawings
using 0.03mm to 1mm black drawing pens, building
upon those lines to create value.
Emiko added color by painting layers of pale watercolor.
She added final details to her illustrations
using drawing pens and colored pencils.

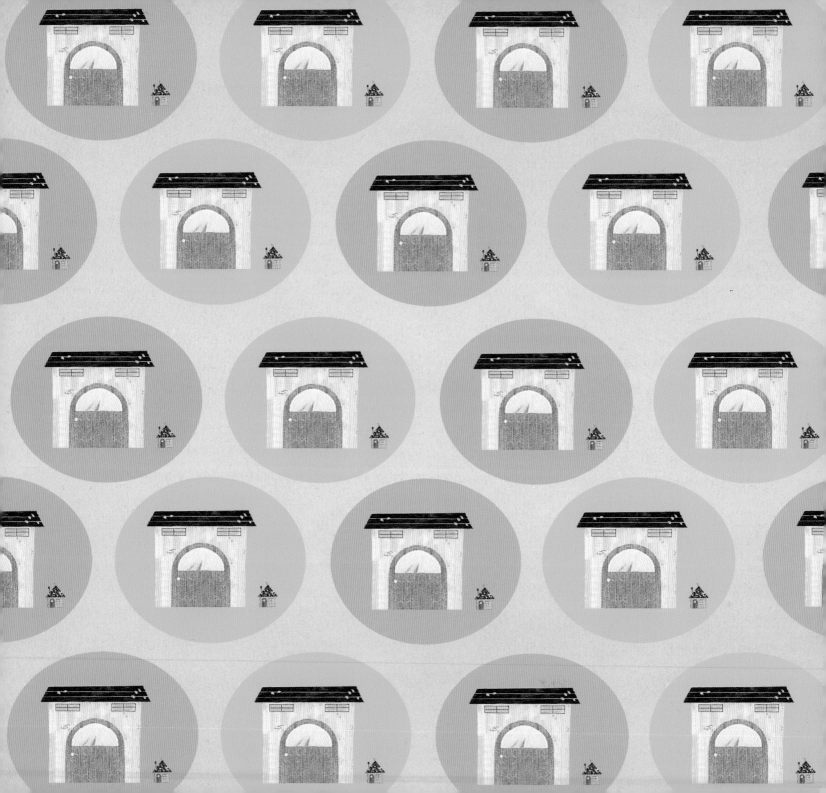